MOTHER GOOSE FAVORITES

SELECTED RHYMES FROM
THE ORIGINAL VOLLAND EDITION

Illustrated by Frederick Richardson

Abridged Edition

DERRYDALE BOOKS
New York

Old Mother Goose, when
  She wanted to wander,
Would ride through the air
  On a very fine gander.

Bah, bah, black sheep,
    Have you any wool?
Yes, marry, have I,
    Three bags full;
One for my master,
    One for my dame,
But none for the little boy
    Who cries in the lane.

To market, to market, to buy a fat pig,
Home again, home again, jiggety, jig.

Pussy cat, pussy cat, where have you been?
I've been to London to see the Queen.
Pussy cat, pussy cat, what did you there?
I frightened a little mouse under the chair.

Old Mother Hubbard
Went to the cupboard
   To get her poor dog a bone;
But when she came there
The cupboard was bare,
   And so the poor dog had none.

This pig went to market,
That pig stayed at home;
This pig had roast meat,
That pig had none;
This pig went to the barn door,
And cried "week, week," for more.

Sing a song of sixpence, a bag full of rye,
Four and twenty blackbirds baked in a pie;
When the pie was opened the birds began to sing,
And wasn't this a dainty dish to set before the king?
The king was in the parlor counting out his money;
The queen was in the kitchen eating bread and honey;
The maid was in the garden hanging out the clothes,
There came a little blackbird and nipped off her nose.

Little Jack Horner
  Sat in a corner
Eating a Christmas pie;
  He put in his thumb,
  And pulled out a plum,
And said: "Oh, what a good boy am I!"

Little Bo-peep has lost her sheep,
And can't tell where to find them;
Leave them alone, and they'll come home,
And bring their tails behind them.

The Queen of Hearts,
She made some tarts
All on a summer's day;
The Knave of Hearts,
He stole those tarts,
And took them clean away.

The King of Hearts
Called for the tarts,
And beat the Knave full sore;
The Knave of Hearts
Brought back the tarts,
And vowed he'd steal no more.

Little Tom Tucker
Sings for his supper.
What shall he eat?
White bread and butter.
How will he cut it
Without e'er a knife?
How will he marry
Without e'er a wife?

There was an old woman who lived in a shoe,
She had so many children she didn't know what to do.
She gave them some broth without any bread,
She whipped them all soundly and put them to bed.

Jack Sprat could eat no fat,
His wife could eat no lean;
So 'twixt them both they cleared the cloth,
And licked the platter clean.

Pat a cake, pat a cake, Baker's man;
So I do, master, as fast as I can.
Pat it and prick it and mark it with T,
And then it will serve for Tommy and me.

Simple Simon met a pieman
  Going to the fair;
Says Simple Simon to the pieman:
  "Pray let me taste your ware."

Says the pieman to Simple Simon:
  "Show me first your penny;"
Says Simple Simon to the pieman:
  "Indeed I have not any."

Humpty Dumpty sat on a wall,
Humpty Dumpty had a great fall;
All the king's horses and all the king's men
Couldn't put Humpty Dumpty together again.

Little Miss Muffet
Sat on a tuffet,
Eating some curds and whey;
There came a great spider,
And sat down beside her,
And frightened Miss Muffet away.

Old King Cole
Was a merry old soul,
And a merry old soul was he;
He called for his pipe,
And he called for his bowl,
And he called for his fiddlers three.

A, B, C, D, E, F, G,
H, I, J, K, L, M, N, O, P,
Q, R, S, and T, U, V,
W, X, and Y and Z.
Now I've said my A, B, C,
Tell me what you think of me.

Pease-porridge hot,
  Pease-porridge cold,
Pease-porridge in the pot
  Nine days old.
Spell me that in four letters;
  I will: T H A T.

Jack, be nimble; Jack, be quick;
Jack, jump over the candlestick.

Dickery, dickery, dock,
The mouse ran up the clock;
The clock struck one,
The mouse ran down,
Dickery, dickery, dock.

Mistress Mary, quite contrary,
How does your garden grow?
With silver bells and cockle shells
And pretty maids all in a row.

Peter, Peter, pumpkin eater,
Had a wife and couldn't keep her;
He put her in a pumpkin shell,
And then he kept her very well.

Peter, Peter, pumpkin eater,
Had another, and didn't love her;
Peter learned to read and spell,
And then he loved her very well.

Jack and Jill went up the hill
    To fetch a pail of water;
Jack fell down and broke his crown,
    And Jill came tumbling after.

Ding–dong–bell, the cat's in the well.
  Who put her in?   Little Johnny Green.
  Who pulled her out?   Great Johnny Stout.
    What a naughty boy was that
    To drown poor pussy cat
  Who never did him any harm,
  And killed the mice in his father's barn.

Wee Willie Winkie runs through the town,
Upstairs and downstairs, in his nightgown;
Tapping at the window, crying at the lock:
"Are the babes in their beds, for it's now ten o'clock?

Hush-a-bye, Baby, upon the tree top,
When the wind blows the cradle will rock;
When the bough breaks the cradle will fall,
Down tumbles cradle and Baby and all.

There were two blackbirds sitting on a hill,
One named Jack and the other named Jill.
Fly away, Jack!   Fly away, Jill!
Come again, Jack!   Come again, Jill!

Little Boy Blue, come blow your horn,
The sheep's in the meadow, the cow's in the corn.
What! Is this the way you mind your sheep,
Under the haycock fast asleep?

As I was going to St. Ives
I met seven wives.
Every wife had seven sacks,
Every sack had seven cats,
Every cat had seven kits.
Kits, cats, sacks and wives,
How many were going to St. Ives?

High diddle diddle,
The cat and the fiddle,
The cow jumped over the moon;
The little dog laughed
To see such craft,
And the dish ran away with the spoon.

Diddle, diddle, dumpling, my son John,
Went to bed with his breeches on,
One stocking off, and one stocking on,
Diddle, diddle, dumpling, my son John.

There was a crooked man,
  And he went a crooked mile,
He found a crooked sixpence
  Against a crooked stile;
He bought a crooked cat
  Which caught a crooked mouse,
And they all lived together
  In a little crooked house.

Polly, put the kettle on,
Polly, put the kettle on,
Polly, put the kettle on,
    We'll all have tea.
Sukey, take it off again,
Sukey, take it off again,
Sukey, take it off again,
    They're all gone away.